Countdown!

Kay Woodward
and Ofra Amit

READZONE

Countdown!

ReadZone Books Limited

First published in this edition 2015

© in this edition ReadZone Books Limited 2015
© in text Kay Woodward 2005
© in illustrations Ofra Amit 2005

Kay Woodward has asserted her right under the Copyright Designs and Patents Act 1988 to be identified as the author of this work.

Ofra Amit has asserted her right under the Copyright Designs and Patents Act 1988 to be identified as the illustrator of this work.

Every attempt has been made by the Publisher to secure appropriate permissions for material reproduced in this book. If there has been any oversight we will be happy to rectify the situation in future editions or reprints. Written submissions should be made to the Publisher.

British Library Cataloguing in Publication Data (CIP) is available for this title.

Printed in Malta by Melita Press.

ISBN 978 1 78322 462 3

Visit our website: www.readzonebooks.com

It's time to go.

Ready for countdown.

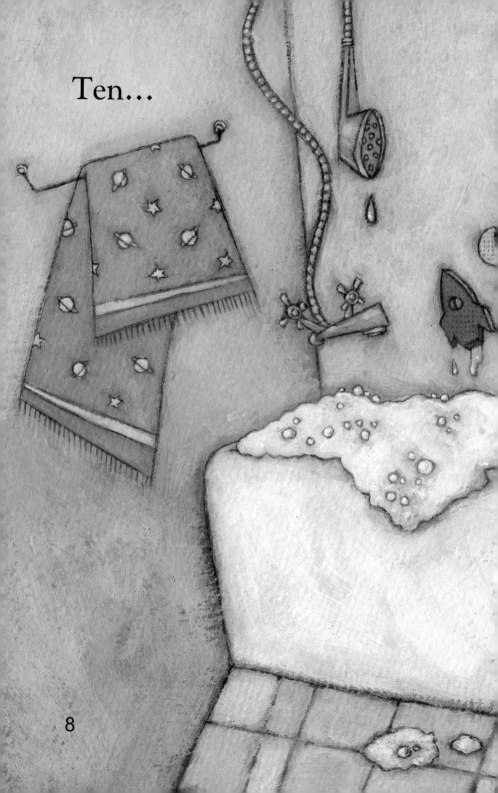

Ten...

...a super-clean astronaut.

Nine…

...a shiny spacesuit.

Eight…

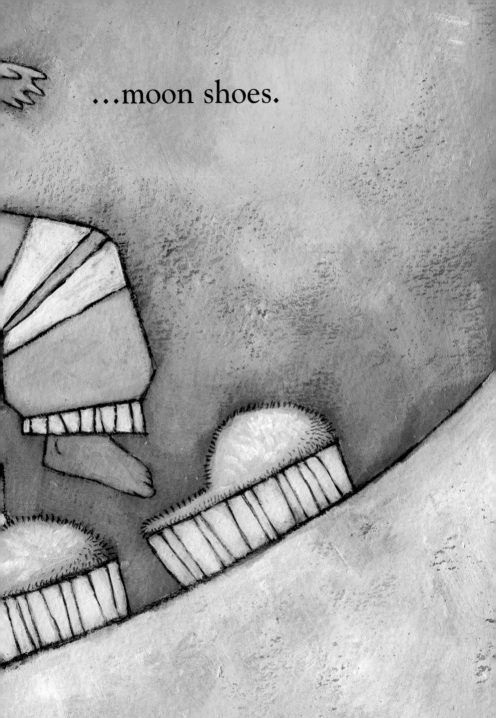

...moon shoes.

Seven...

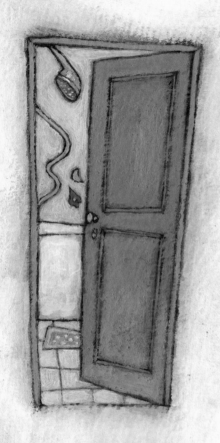

...a rocket book.

Six...

…space juice.

Five…

...a clever co-pilot.

19

Four...

...a helmet.

21

Three...

…galactic goggles.

Two…

...a walkie-talkie.

One...

...here's my spaceship.

Zero...

ZZZzzzzz!

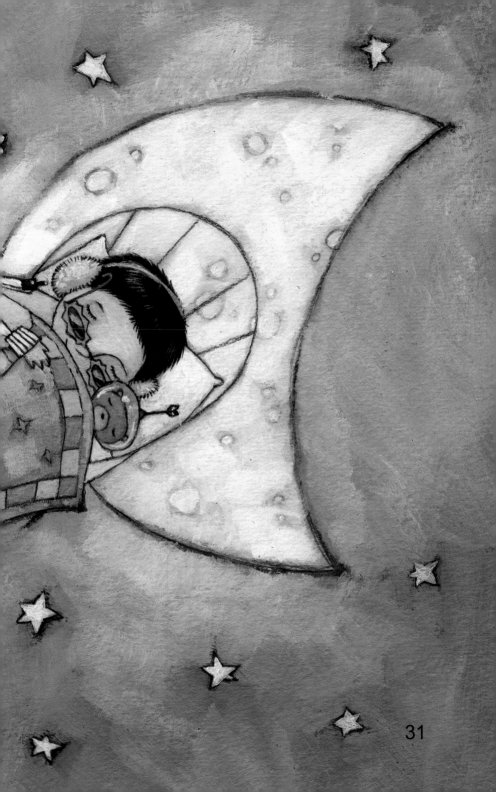

Did you enjoy this book?

Look out for more *Robins* titles –
first stories in only 50 words

A Head Full of Stories by Su Swallow and Tim Archbold
ISBN 978 1 78322 456 2

Billy on the Ball by Paul Harrison and Silvia Raga
ISBN 978 1 78322 125 7

Countdown! by Kay Woodward and Ofra Amit
ISBN 978 1 78322 462 3

Cave-Baby and the Mammoth by Vivian French and Lisa Williams
ISBN 978 1 78322 126 4

Hattie the Dancing Hippo by Jillian Powell and Emma Dodson
ISBN 978 1 78322 463 0

Molly is New by Nick Turpin and Silvia Raga
ISBN 978 1 78322 455 5

Mr Bickle and the Ghost by Stella Gurney and Silvia Raga
ISBN 978 1 78322 472 2

Noisy Books by Paul Harrison and Fabiano Fiorin
ISBN 978 1 78322 464 7

Not-So-Silly Sausage by Stella Gurney and Liz Million
ISBN 978 1 78322 465 4

The Sand Dragon by Su Swallow and Silvia Raga
ISBN 978 1 78322 127 1

Undersea Adventure by Paul Harrison and Barbara Nascimbeni
ISBN 978 1 78322 466 1

Yummy Scrummy by Paul Harrison and Belinda Worsley
ISBN 978 1 78322 467 8